This igloo book belongs to:

....

igloobooks

Published in 2020
by Igloo Books Ltd
Cottage Farm
Sywell
NN6 0BJ
www.igloobooks.com

Copyright © 2014 Igloo Books Ltd
Igloo Books is an imprint of Bonnier Books UK

0620 004
12 14 15 13 11
ISBN 978-1-78197-623-4

Illustrated by Matthew Scott

Printed and manufactured in China

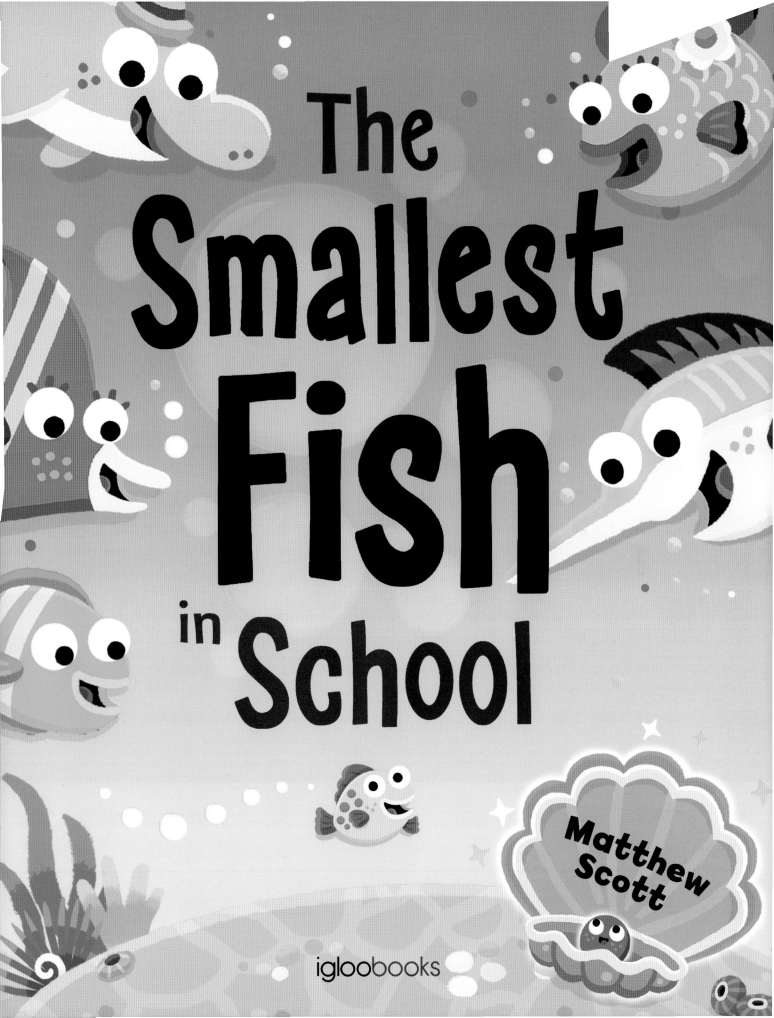

The Smallest Fish in School

Matthew Scott

igloobooks

DING-A-LING!

It was lunchtime at Mr Crab's School for Fish.
"Race you to the fish food," said Spike the
swordfish to Danny the dolphin.

"WAIT FOR ME!"
cried Little Fish,
as he swam along behind.

Little Fish **waggled** his
tail and **wiggled** his fins,
but he couldn't keep up.

swoosh!

Everyone darted off.

They **gobbled** up the fish food,
chomp, chomp, chomp.

"I'm FED UP of being small,"
said Little Fish, sadly.

Soon, lunchtime was over. "This afternoon, we're going to study the coral reef," said Mr Crab.

Danny and Spike thought that sounded boring.
"We want to see something **exciting**," they said.

While Mr Crab was talking about seahorses, Danny and Spike snuck off to explore.

Danny and Spike
disappeared into the ship.
"WAIT FOR ME!"
shouted Little Fish.

Suddenly,
he heard a cry,
"HELP! HELP!"

Danny and Spike were about
to be eaten by a shark!

"LEAVE MY FRIENDS ALONE!"
cried Little Fish, angrily.

"There's NOTHING wrong with being small,"

said Little Fish.

"Pick on someone
your OWN size,
you BIG BULLY."

Little Fish flicked his tail.
He **wiggled** and **waggled**.
Then he darted, **swoosh**,
through a porthole.

SNAP,
SNAP,
went the shark.

Then, suddenly, he got
stuck!

Danny and Spike swam back to Mr Crab.
"Little Fish saved us from the shark!" they cried.

"THREE CHEERS for
BRAVE Little Fish,"
said Mr Crab.

Little Fish may have been the smallest fish in the class, but he was the **biggest** hero in the school.